Always the Elf

Story by Kimberly Jensen

Illustrations by Glenn Harmon

ISBN 13: 978-1-59955-086-2

Published by CFI, an imprint of Cedar Fort, Inc.
2373 W. 700 S., Springville, UT, 84663
Distributed by Cedar Fort, Inc., www.cedarfort.com

LIBRARY OF CONGRESS CATALOGING-IN-PUBLICATION DATA

Jensen, Kimberly.
  Always the elf / written by Kimberly Jensen; illustrated by Glenn Harmon.
    p. cm.
  Summary: When second-grader Tasia complains to her mother about always
having to be an elf in the school Christmas pageant, her mother tells her a
story that makes her realize the importance of Santa's elves.
  ISBN 978-1-59955-086-2
  [1. Elves—Fiction. 2. Jesus Christ—Nativity—Fiction. 3.
Christmas—Fiction.] I. Harmon, Glenn, ill. II. Title.

  PZ7.J4346Al 2007
  [E]—dc22

              2007025266

Jacket and book design by Nicole Williams
Edited by Lyndsee Simpson Cordes
Cover design © 2007 by Lyle Mortimer
Printed on acid-free paper

Printed in the United States
10 9 8 7 6 5 4 3 2 1

Author Dedication

To Tasia, Clayton, and Bennett, my inspiration, Mark, my motivation,
and to my mom and dad, my biggest fans.

Artist Dedication

To Max—I hope you always remember the true reason for Christmas.

Tasia got off the bus and stamped through the mud puddles as she walked the block between the bus stop and home. It was a Tuesday just like any other winter day. Melted snow formed muddy pools of water on the pavement.

She threw open the front door and stomped through the kitchen, making sure her arrival would not go unnoticed. She tossed her backpack on the floor, kicked off her boots, and plopped down, belly first, on the couch in the family room. She let out a loud sigh that could not be ignored by her mother in the next room.

"How was your day?" Tasia's mother asked.

"Umph" was all that Tasia could reply.

"By the look on your face, I can tell it was not one of your best days in second grade."

"Mom, it's just not fair! I'm always the elf!"

"What do you mean 'always the elf'?"

"Tryouts for the school Christmas program were today, and once again I've been picked to be the elf. I really wanted to be the ballerina or the teddy bear. I would have even liked to be the toy soldier, but, as always, I'm the elf."

"Being the elf is a special role," Mom said as she sat on the couch next to Tasia. "Elves have a very important role in Christmas. In fact, without them, Christmas would be very different."

"I don't care," Tasia pouted. "Katie gets to be the ballerina, and Brianna got picked to be the teddy bear. They get to wear fancy costumes when all I get to wear is this dumb green hat that doesn't even fit my head."

"May I see it?" asked Mom.

"If you want. It's no big deal," Tasia said, pulling a rumpled felt hat from the bottom of her backpack and handing it to her mom.

"Hmm, how interesting," said Mom, turning the hat around in her hands and stroking the brim.

"What's so interesting about it?" Tasia asked sourly.

"Well, I've heard about these hats, but I've never seen one quite like this. It's been a long time, but I think I can remember how the story goes."

"What story?" Tasia asked, showing a little more interest in the rumpled green hat.

"Well, it happened a long time ago, before television and Playstation and even before Barbie, I think."

"Okay, Mom, I get the picture. It was a really, really long, long time ago."

"Okay then." Mom started again.

A long time ago, there was a village nestled deep in the woods. Very few people knew about this small village where families of elves lived. The tiny elves lived ordinary lives behind the protection of the forest's walls. They didn't have magical powers or pockets full of stardust. Their bodies may have been tiny, but their hearts were huge and beat faster than the hearts of any other creature on the earth. If you looked really close, you could see their hearts beating right through their tiny jumpers, just as if their hearts were dancing on top of their skin.

The elves spent their days making beautiful buttons of all sorts. Soft buttons, hard buttons, shiny buttons, colorful buttons, and even animal-shaped buttons. They decorated their houses with buttons too. Button plates, button picture frames, button chairs. They wore buttons on all of their clothes and shoes. They even wore button hats.

The elves busied themselves during the day making buttons, and at night they delivered those buttons all over the world. The elves were very careful to be sure all of the buttons were delivered to the right places. They counted the buttons and made sure that not one was missing or broken. Then the buttons were wrapped up in packages and sent off with the delivery elves who took them to shoe and clothing factories far and wide.

There was a special delivery elf named Brams. He didn't have any brothers or sisters. He only remembers his mother's smell, not her face. She smelled of freshly cut wood on a rainy day, with a touch of maple syrup. As he worked, he smiled and tried hard to remember her face. The last time he saw her he was eleven years old. His mother and father left the house one day and never returned. Brams never knew exactly what happened to them, only that they had moved on to a better place.

After his parents disappeared, another family adopted Brams. They had a boy named Tucker who was just a year younger than Brams. The boys became brothers by fate and best friends by choice. They spent their days exploring the forest floors, trees, brooks, and valleys. They swung tree branches like swords and proclaimed their right to royal land. They made helmets out of pine boughs and spoke to the critters of the forest, who answered them with whoops, chitters, and cah-cahs.

But as all little boys do, Brams and Tucker quickly grew up and were forced to find their way in the world. Tucker became a designer in the button factory, and there he met a beautiful girl elf. Soon they were married and had five little elves to care for.

The house where Brams lived was surrounded by trees, all bending to the north. His little house was nestled in the trees in a valley where the winds never stopped breathing. It was the winds that kept the trees bending to the north. Brams lived alone in the little house with round windows. He thought that the circle-shaped windows greeted his guests like the smiles of porcelain dolls.

He had discovered the house one day while he was out collecting shiny pebbles to be shaped and sculpted into fine buttons. No one wanted to live in the old, falling-down house in the middle of the forest. It had not been torn down, just left to itself, surrounded by trees.

Brams went right to work, making the shack into a home. He scrubbed the sticky sap from the tin roof until it sparkled like silver in the sun. He cut down trees and replaced the rotting boards on the back of the house. He made another round window on the east side of the house so that when the sun rose each morning, Bram's would feel its rays shining on his face, which would be on the pillow, on the bed, set precisely where the sun would warm his right cheek, just so, to wake him ever so slowly to greet the new day.

More than anything, Brams loved collecting things. One of his favorite things to collect was fabric. His collection was growing quickly, and Brams loved to admire the different fabrics.

Just about everyone in the village worked for the button factory. Brams started out as a collector of raw materials. He spent his days in the forest, collecting items that could be made into buttons. He hunted for wood, stone, clay, and sand. He was such a hard worker that he soon became the head button designer and got to work with his brother Tucker. But Brams quickly grew weary of being inside the factory all day where the sun never hit his face. He asked for a job delivering buttons instead.

Brams was excited about his new job. He loved visiting different places every day and delivering beautiful buttons to factories all over the world. He never tired of the oohs and ahhs as he opened his pack and showed the latest buttons to his eager buyers. When he traveled, he always looked for new fabrics to add to his collection.

His travels allowed him to explore new countries and landscapes to collect amazing materials that weren't found in his small forest. His journeys took him to the east, where he collected fine silks, bamboo, and spices. The silk would be used to cover buttons. These buttons would add a splash of color to an ordinary jacket. The bamboo would be carved into fine buttons for ladies' dresses, and the spices would be ground up to make a sticky mixture that the elves poured into button molds shaped like beautiful birds.

He collected fabric from islands that held the brightest colors he had ever seen. The plants of the rainforest fascinated Brams, and when the plants were dried, the elves made lovely green buttons shaped like banana leaves.

To the north, he found timber with unique knots and rings in the wood. The wood made fantastic buckles for shoes.

To the south, he found sands of all colors that the elves melted to create beautiful glass buttons worn by kings.

He collected gems and crystals of all shapes and sizes. He brought home shiny rocks and pebbles and pieces of glass. He rummaged through the city streets, looking for anything shiny he could carry home in the knapsack he always carried with him. Brams saw the beauty in other peoples' throwaways. He saw possibility in things that most people wouldn't even notice.

Brams had learned not to share his treasures with others. They often teased him for collecting what they called garbage. But Brams created masterpieces on the small wood table in the middle of his house.

It was at this table in his lovely little house that the artist came to life. He happily cut and chiseled and sanded and buffed and polished.

One night, when Brams was exploring a factory to which he had delivered his ever-popular bird-shaped buttons, he came across a large piece of green felt fabric that had been tossed in the trash. There wasn't anything special about the fabric. It didn't shimmer in the moonlight, and it didn't have any pretty patterns on it, but Brams thought he might make good use of it, so he dragged it home. He soon forgot about the ordinary fabric as his travels took him to exotic sewing shops full of wonderful material that glowed in the sun and was covered in unusual patterns.

Several months later, Brams was making a delivery to a town he had never been to before. He took his buttons to the local factory and was about to leave when he saw donkeys and camels and a crowd of people gathered around a dark cave. Since he was so small, Brams moved silently to the front of the crowd and gazed into the dark cave. There he saw three of the most glorious people he had ever seen in his life: a mother and a father and their newborn baby boy lying in a manger. "Who is he?" Brams wondered aloud.

"He's the King of Kings, the Lord of Hosts, the Son of God," whispered a small shepherd boy, without taking his eyes off the magnificent scene in front of him.

"The Son of God, here in this stable?" Brams thought to himself. He could not believe that his travels had brought him to the very stable where the Savior was sleeping in the arms of his mother, Mary. Brams watched as Mary cooed to the babe in her arms, and he moved closer to get a glimpse of the little one. He watched the babe move his arms and scrunch up his face at the sounds of the small crowd. Brams felt a warm tingle start at his toes, move up to his heart, and then tickle his cheeks. He had never felt such peace in all his life.

Brams hurried back to his village and told the story of the birth of the Christ Child to everyone in town. The elves decided they needed to give a very special gift to the babe in the manger. They gathered many gifts for the Savior: shoes, hats, blankets, gold, and all sorts of beautiful trinkets and buttons. But as Brams looked at all of the gifts, he didn't feel right about any of them.

Then Brams's heart began to beat faster, and a smile grew on his face, extending from ear to ear. "I have the perfect gift," Brams said quietly. "The Christ Child would expect no greater gift than for us to love each other. We can show one another our love by doing kind things and always using kind words." The crowd nodded in agreement.

Brams ran to his house and dragged out the old piece of rumpled green felt he had collected a few months before. But today it seemed to hold a beauty he hadn't seen before. He ran back to the crowd and held it up for all to see. "This green is the sign of God's great love for us, and we will wear it every day to help us remember Him," Brams announced.

That piece of rumpled green felt was made into thousands of tiny green hats. The elves wore the hats as they performed good deeds every day.

It was several hundred years later that Santa Claus showed up in the town and hired the elves to help him at the North Pole. They still wear those same green hats and perform kind deeds each and every day, not just on Christmas.

"So you see," Mom finished, "always being the elf is one of the greatest roles of all."

"I suppose it is," Tasia said with a smile. She gently picked up the green felt hat, placed it on her head, and whispered to herself, "Always the elf."